The Big Chase

WENDY GRAHAM

ILLUSTRATED BY IAN FORSS

sundance

A Haights Cross Communications Company

Published by
Sundance Publishing
234 Taylor Street
Littleton, MA 01460

Copyright © text Wendy Graham
Copyright © illustrations Ian Forss
Project commissioned and managed by
Lorraine Bambrough-Kelly, The Writer's Style
Designed by Cath Lindsey/design rescue

First published 1998 by
Addison Wesley Longman Australia Pty Limited
95 Coventry Street
South Melbourne 3205 Australia
Exclusive United States Distribution: Sundance Publishing

ISBN 0-7608-3283-8

Printed In Canada

Contents

CHAPTER 1

The Wolfman Mystery

Paula gasped. Her brother Todd was balanced on the very top of the monkey bars, waving a piece of paper.

"Listen, everybody!" Todd shouted.

Nobody in the schoolyard took much notice.

"I said *listen*!" he yelled louder.

Some of the children stopped what they were doing and looked up at Todd.

"Have you all read this?" he called, waving the paper. It was the school newsletter, *The Bulletin*.

There were murmurs of "Yes" and "No" and "What is it?"

Todd held up his hand like a traffic policeman. "Listen," he said. And he began to read.

The Bulletin

Madison Elementary School

The Wolfman Mystery

It's time again for the annual field trip to Echo Lake. As we all know, every year a strange creature known as "The Wolfman" appears at our picnic, running through the picnic area and surrounding park. He is known to be harmless (so far), but he always causes a great deal of excitement.

This year, *The Madison Community News* is sending along a reporter to photograph The Wolfman and to write a story about him. If anybody is able to catch The Wolfman, the newspaper is offering a choice of prizes: a pair of in-line skates, a skateboard, or a basketball.

Can *you* solve The Wolfman Mystery?

Todd folded the newsletter and put it in his pocket. "This year," he announced, "we *are* going to catch The Wolfman!"

A commotion filled the schoolyard. There were shouts and groans and cries of "No way!"

"Wait, wait, listen!" shouted Todd. He paused, waiting for the kids to pay attention.

Todd continued. "Yes!" he cried. "I've got a plan! This year we'll catch him! We'll trick him and trip him and trap him, and one of us will win the prize!"

An excited murmur rumbled through the crowd.

"And we'll find out who he is!" Todd finished, throwing his cap into the air. Then he grasped the railing of the monkey bars and somersaulted down.

Kids squealed and jumped around and slapped hands with each other, shouting, "Yes!"

Paula joined in the excitement, dancing around with her friends. But what plan could her brother have?

CHAPTER 2

The Bus of Excitement

The buses cruised along the highway to Echo Lake.

Todd, in the first bus, threw rolled-up paper spitballs that went splat on the bus ceiling . . . and stuck there. His friends roared with laughter.

Mr. Franklin, the physical education teacher, frowned at the children, trying to discover why they were laughing. He failed to glance up at the bus ceiling. This sent them all into fresh peals of laughter.

"Now, children," Mr. Franklin said. "Attention, please. There's to be no misbehavior on the way to Echo Lake. Last year a certain person . . . ," he paused and looked directly at Todd, "let a live frog out of a jar in the middle of the bus trip."

Giggles rippled through the bus.

"Silence!" commanded Mr. Franklin, and all became quiet again.

Quiet, until Sui-Chan rolled marbles down the bus floor, and then blamed Katya Ivovic.

And Fraser Morris was sick all over himself and his best friend, who was sitting next to him. Well, his former best friend, that is.

Then Theo Papadopoulos stood up when he shouldn't have, and whacked his head on the overhead bar. An awesome lump erupted immediately.

And all the way to Echo Lake, everybody talked about The Wolfman.

"Remember last year? Remember how he shinnied up that tree and nobody knew where he went?"

"What about the year before when he had a false beard!"

"Perhaps he's a mad old hermit!"

"Maybe he's a crazy millionaire, and owns Echo Lake!"

The excitement grew. Now and then, there'd be a shout, "There he is!" And everyone would crane their necks to see out of the bus windows.

It might have been a glimpse of a deer bounding among the bushes. It might have been a glimpse of a fox running through the undergrowth. Or it *might* have been a glimpse of The Wolfman, racing alongside the bus among the trees, laughing his wild cackle.

CHAPTER 3

An Anxious Wait

The bus jerked to a stop, and the children jostled their way off.

Paula and Katya ran to the adventure playground.

Fraser and Sui-Chan began a game of baseball with some friends.

Todd and Theo climbed a tree and hung upside down from a branch. Mr. Franklin came rushing over. "Come down from there at once!" he shouted. "Carefully!"

The reporter from the local newspaper took a photo.

Tents and wooden picnic tables were put up. Some parents, who had come to help, heated up food in the community hall's kitchen.

Soon the tables were overloaded with lasagna, spring rolls, salads, crackers and cheese, rice cakes, and fresh rolls. The barbecue was lit, and the hot dogs smoked and sizzled.

Mr. Franklin banged a gong, and there was a rush for the food. Paula, Todd, Theo, Sui-Chan, Fraser, and Katya sat in a group. They ate and laughed and sang silly songs.

They talked about the newspaper article
and the prizes for the person who managed
to catch The Wolfman.

"I'd choose the in-line skates," announced
Katya.

"Me, too!" chorused Sui-Chan and Fraser.

"I'd rather have the basketball," said Theo.

Todd took up a stance, arms outstretched, as if he was riding a skateboard. "I'd pick the skateboard," he said, "and enter all the skating competitions."

At a slight noise in the bushes, they glanced around quickly. Fraser gasped. Sui-Chan held her breath. Paula felt a little knot in her stomach. Was it The Wolfman? Todd exchanged glances with Theo.

A huge crow strutted into view. The children laughed at their fears.

But where was The Wolfman? Would they *really* be able to catch him this year? Was Todd right?

CHAPTER 4

There He Is!

GRR! GRR!

Paula jumped with fright.

They heard his roar before they saw him. Paula's heart began to hammer.

The Wolfman looked scary. He wore a dark hat pulled down over his head and eyes and a big, brown, hairy overcoat. From nowhere at all, he leaped into sight and ran among the children, screaming wildly.

Then he streaked across the picnic area, as fast as a jackrabbit.

The air filled with squeals and shrieks and whoops of joy, as the children thundered across the park after him. Some of the teachers joined in the chase, and a few of the parents did, too.

The Wolfman dashed away, his hairy overcoat flying out behind him. His head low, he crashed through the bushes and raced down the winding gravel path. Birds took flight, squawking, and stones sprayed up as he ran.

Paula could hear him breathing in great, gulping gasps.

Then he paused, just for a second, and shook himself, looking around at the children. With a wild shriek, he threw something toward them and bounded away again, along the path.

The children pounced on it. It was a note, wrapped around a lollipop. Todd spread out the paper and read aloud:

You can run all you like,
as fast as you can.
But you'll never catch up
to the MaD WOLFMaN!

Sui-Chan shouted. "Where did he go?" The children wandered around looking everywhere.

Suddenly, there was a terrible roar right behind them. Paula squealed and covered her eyes. The Wolfman ran straight through their midst, his wild laugh echoing over his shoulder. He leaped over fallen logs and burst through the bushes, occasionally glancing over his shoulder.

Again the children took up the chase, and some of the teachers and a few of the parents joined in.

"Look! Another message!" This time Katya picked it up and read aloud:

I'm the Echo Lake Mystery. You can run all you like, but you'll never catch me.

The children gasped as they heard the crackle of a twig up ahead.

Was it him? Off they ran again.

CHAPTER 5

A Trick and a Trap

Everyone was chasing The Wolfman. Everyone, that is, except Todd and Theo. Instead, they were waiting, hiding on the other side of the lake. Waiting to trick and trip and trap The Wolfman.

They could hear the shouts as he
approached. There he was!

Todd, from behind a tree, put out his leg and tripped The Wolfman, and at the same time Theo pounced.

The three struggled together. Paula, Sui-Chan, Katya, Fraser, and the rest of the children gathered around, trying to get a glimpse of The Wolfman's face.

Todd grabbed one of The Wolfman's arms, and Theo grabbed his leg. They all rolled together for a few seconds. There were grunts and muffled groans and a cry of "Ouch!" but Todd and Theo held on tight. They had tricked him and tripped him and trapped him, and they weren't going to let him go!

Then, with a sudden thunderous roar, The Wolfman shook off their grips. He rushed away, shrieking, arms outstretched.

And without looking back, he took a giant leap—and splashed right into Echo Lake!

Everyone stood, gaping, shocked into silence.

The children knew better than to go in the water after him. They watched helplessly as The Wolfman swam with powerful strokes through the murky water.

They ran around the edge of the lake, trying to keep him in sight.

Soon the lake was calm and still. There was no sign of The Wolfman.

The children searched the boathouses by the lake, and they lifted the overturned rowboats and looked under them.

They lay on the wooden planks of the dock to peer underneath, where the water gently lapped the giant pilings.

And they scanned the branches of the trees that lined the water's edge.

It was no use. The Wolfman had disappeared. And now they would never know who he was.

CHAPTER 6

A Surprise and a Secret

"Look!" somebody shouted. There, floating on the lake, like a dark puddle of spilled paint, was The Wolfman's brown, hairy overcoat.

Todd fished it out with a stick.

They took it back to the picnic area and spread it on the ground to dry.

"Well, we *nearly* caught him," Todd said.

"I had hold of his leg!" said Theo.

"You were scared," Fraser teased Paula.

Paula nodded. She *had* been scared.
"Weren't you?" she asked her brother.

Todd nodded, too.

"Well, so was I," said Fraser.

The group, along with the rest of their friends, laughed and sang silly songs and talked. Who could tell? Maybe *next* year they'd catch The Wolfman!

Todd and Theo went searching for frogs. Katya, Fraser, and Sui-Chan began playing baseball.

Others played volleyball or tag.

Some balanced on the wobbling rope ladder, and others whooshed through the air on the space trolley.

They all seemed to have forgotten about The Wolfman. Except for Paula. She hadn't forgotten him, and she was worried. The Wolfman couldn't have drowned, could he? What if none of the teachers knew he'd disappeared into the lake?

She hurried up to a couple of the teachers. "The Wolfman jumped into the lake!" she told them.

The teachers laughed. The newspaper reporter laughed, too, and wrote in his notebook.

Paula moved away. It looked like nobody would win one of those special prizes, after all. And nobody seemed too worried about what had happened to The Wolfman.
Except her.

With a sigh, Paula stepped into the shade of a tent. And that's when she saw an amazing sight. Something she would never have believed if she hadn't seen it with her own eyes. Something she decided to keep as her very own secret.

He was inside the tent, sitting on a chair. There was a blanket around his shoulders, and people were fussing over him. He had his shoes off, and his big white feet were shivering.

It was Mr. Franklin, and he was dripping wet from head to toe!

ABOUT THE AUTHOR

Wendy Graham

Wendy has always loved reading and writing. When she was a young child, she realized that she'd read every children's book in the local library. So, what did she do? She started writing her own books!

As an adult, Wendy began writing short stories and articles for newspapers and magazines. While taking a course in professional writing and editing, she decided that what she really liked to do was write for children. Wendy says that when writing children's stories, she can use her imagination and dreams and wishes to make everything come true—on paper!

Wendy works full-time, writing new material and looking after her family, her pets, and a rambling garden.

ABOUT THE ILLUSTRATOR

Ian Forss

In 1969, when Ian Forss was nine years old, his mother commented that a picture he had drawn looked "nice." That was all the encouragement he needed. From then on, he was always to be found drawing pictures.

Ian drew all the way through college as he earned a degree in Art and Design. And when he went on to earn a graduate degree in Film and Television, he was still drawing.

Today, Ian lives with his wife, Linda, and two children, Jade and James. He enjoys riding his horse, Apache, even if sometimes it makes drawing steady lines a bit tricky.